D1410850

# A Pony for Keeps

## Elizabeth Henning Sutton
### Photographs by Mary Brant Gamma

THOMASSON-GRANT
Charlottesville, Virginia

Dedicated to Jefferson

Copyright © 1991 by Thomasson-Grant, Inc. All rights reserved.
Text copyright © 1991 by Elizabeth Henning Sutton.
Photographs copyright © 1991 by Mary Brant Gamma.

This book, or any portions thereof, may not be reproduced in any form without written permission of the publisher, Thomasson-Grant, Inc.

Printed in the United States.

Author's acknowledgment:  For E.Y.S., D.G.S., and F.T.S., in memory of Milkshake.

Photographer's acknowledgment:  With love and appreciation to Captain Tacot for inspiration, to R.W.G. for believing in me, and to Mother and Father for allowing me to follow a dream.

Special thanks to L.J.C. and Midway Farm and to R.S.M. and Foxcroft Farm.

98  97  96  95  94  93  92          5  4  3

Library of Congress Cataloging-in-Publication Data

Sutton, Elizabeth Henning
     A pony for keeps / Elizabeth Henning Sutton : photographs by Mary Brant Gamma.
          p.     cm.
     Summary : When Meg turns seven she takes riding lessons and receives her own pony.
     ISBN 0-934738-77-7
     [1. Ponies--Fiction.  2. Horsemanship--Fiction.]  I. Gamma, Mary Brant, ill.   II. Title.
     PZ7.S96815Po   1991
     [Fic]--dc20                              90-24435
                                                  CIP
                                                   AC

Thomasson-Grant, Inc.
One Morton Drive, Suite 500
Charlottesville, Virginia 22901
(804) 977-1780

It was the night before Meg's birthday, and her father was reading her a bedtime story. While she was listening, her mind kept wandering to thoughts of what was going to happen in the morning.

Later, she could not get to sleep. Tomorrow she was going to her first riding lesson. For as long as she could remember, Meg had been asking her parents for a pony of her own. But no matter what, they always had the same reply. "No. Not until you are old enough to learn how to ride and care for a pony. Having a pony is a big responsibility. It is more than just a pet or a toy."

So, Meg had waited. She would sit by the fence and watch while her older brother, David, learned to ride.

She envied him for the pony he got for his seventh birthday.

Meg had watched the older children grooming their ponies. It looked like so much fun to stroke their glossy coats and feed them carrots and apples. With thoughts like these, Meg finally fell asleep.

The next morning, at last, it was her seventh birthday. It was autumn, and the weather was just right for being outdoors. Meg's mother drove her to her first riding lesson at Joan's farm.

When they got there, Meg spotted a little pony in a field. The pony came right up to her looking for a treat. Meg had seen the other ponies at Joan's before, but this one was new to her. "He's so cute! I hope I can ride him today," Meg thought to herself.

Just then Joan came along and said, "Hello, Meg. Would you like to help me catch Jefferson? Here are some oats." They offered him the feed bucket.

Joan put a halter on the pony and led him to the stall where he and Meg could get to know each other.

"Jefferson's a good size for you, Meg. Would you like to ride him today?" Meg was too excited to answer. She had waited so long for this moment that she could hardly believe it was real.

They led Jefferson to the barnyard to get him ready to ride. Joan showed Meg how to curry and brush the pony to get him nice and clean before putting on the saddle and bridle. Meg learned to adjust the bit and tighten the girth.

With her helmet fastened and a boost from Joan, she was in the saddle at last. Meg listened carefully as Joan explained the correct way to hold the reins and how to keep her heels down and her feet firmly in the stirrups. Joan seemed to know just the right words to tell Meg how to do everything. There was so much to remember!

As Joan led Jefferson toward the ring, Meg felt his body moving beneath her. It was so much fun to ride. She loved looking ahead through the pony's fuzzy ears, and the smell of his warm, woolly coat.

Next, Joan put the pony on a long line and let
Meg walk him in a circle.  Soon Meg learned to hold
on with her legs and guide herself.  She couldn't wait
to learn to trot.  She felt proud and confident with
Joan helping her.

In the weeks that followed, Meg eagerly looked forward to her lessons at the farm. Christmas was coming, and soon the ponies would have their vacation for the winter. Meg wanted to learn fast.

One Saturday morning Meg arrived a little early for her lesson. She wanted to put the pony's halter on all by herself. But when she went to Jefferson's stall he wasn't there. Meg was sure something was wrong.

Joan saw Meg searching for the pony, and she tried to explain. "Meg, I have something to tell you that you won't want to hear."

"Where is Jefferson?" Meg asked.

"He is still out in the field. Today will be your last lesson with him."

Meg could not believe it. Her mind spun with questions. "Where is he going? Why?"

"I'm moving away, and Jefferson will be going with me," said Joan. "Jefferson is so old now that I couldn't bear to sell him. He deserves a rest from lessons. My little boy will take care of him. Why don't we go find him now, and after your ride today you can say goodbye."

16

The little pony watched them coming toward him.  He seemed to know that this would be his last ride with his new little friend.  He would miss Meg's kind care and regular treats.  But sometimes ponies, and people, have to change homes.  Everyone was very sad.

Joan told the children that she had arranged for them to ride at another farm. "You remember Amy? She has taught here with me before. She will enjoy helping you learn, just as I have. Don't worry, we will surely be together again before long." Meg tried very hard not to cry. She felt terrible, and so did the rest of Joan's students. Meg was sure that no one could take Joan's place. She knew that there was no other pony as nice as Jefferson.

Later, after Meg got home, she tried to imagine what Jefferson would do, far away from the home he had known for so long. She asked her brother, "Do animals think?"

"Of course they do," David said.

"Well, when Jefferson has been away for a while, do you think he'll remember me?"

"I don't know."

Their mother overheard them as she came into the room. "What's the matter? You two look as if you'd lost your best friend!"

"We did!" cried Meg, and she buried her face in her hands.

"You'll find another pony you like, I promise you," Meg's mother said as cheerfully as she could. "Jefferson will be so happy in his new home, and just think, he'll be able to relax every day."

"But who will give him carrots?  And brush him?  Joan's little boy is too young to do those things.  He needs someone like me!"

"Don't worry, Meg.  Joan will look out for him."

A week later, Meg and David went out to visit Amy's farm. The sky was full of clouds, and the wind felt cold. They shivered as they looked at the big barn and all the horses grazing nearby.

Amy was busy teaching a student on a brown pony, and there were many families Meg had never met.

"This is nice," said Meg's mother.

"I don't like it here," answered Meg. "I don't see any little ponies–they're all big. I want a tiny pony like Jefferson." She was thinking, "And a pony of my own."

Meg looked down to find a little white puppy bumping into her leg. As she stooped to pick him up, she didn't see what was coming up the drive to the barn. The children looked up.

It was a horse trailer! Everyone gathered to see who was coming. Two people got out. No one seemed to know who they were. The children heard stomping and whinnying from inside the trailer. Meg walked closer as they began to unload. "Are you Meg?" said the man.

"That's me."

"Well, I think we have a surprise for you!"

Meg watched them lower the ramp.

Looking through the side door of the trailer, Meg saw a little white nose and two dark eyes.

"A pony!" she cried. "She's beautiful!"

The pony backed down the ramp, and the lady handed the lead rope to Meg. Meg's mother smiled. "She's all yours! Would you like to show her her new home?" Meg couldn't say a word.

As Meg led her pony up to the barn, the other children crowded near to look. "Her name is Lady Jane," said Meg's mother. "She is an early Christmas present from Dad and me."

Meg could not stop looking at her new friend. She was the prettiest pony in the whole world. "Thanks!" she cried.

Amy invited her to join a lesson, so as quickly as they could, Meg and her mother put on Lady Jane's saddle and bridle. They checked the stirrups for the right length, and soon Meg was riding all by herself, right into the ring.

Amy was helpful and friendly, and there was another little girl just Meg's age. Amy's farm will be a fine place to ride, thought Meg.

She thought about Jefferson, and hoped he was happy, too.

Meg had many adventures to look forward to with Lady Jane.

At last, Meg's dream had come true. She had a pony to love and care for, a pony to ride any time she wanted, a pony all her own–a pony for *keeps!*

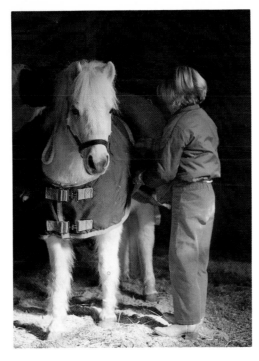

"I love you," Meg whispered as
she gave Lady Jane a pat on her
soft, white nose.